Welcome To Prophetic Ministry

A Practical Interactive Guide To Hearing
God's Voice For Yourself and Others

Cathy Greer

MSN Ministries

Mission Viejo, California USA

Copyright © 2017 by **Cathy Greer**

We reserve the right to allow you to copy any portion of this you want. Teach others, train and equip with any part of this book.

Cathy Greer/MSN Ministries

25108 Marguerite Prkway

Mission Viejo, California 92692

www.msnministries.com

I dedicate this book to my loving savior Jesus Christ and to my loving husband Stuart. To my beautiful daughter Stephanie may you walk in the fullness of His love and exercise your spiritual gifts for His glory.

"But he who prophesies speaks edification, exhortation and comfort to men."

—CORINTHIANS 14:1-3 NIV

Contents

Friendship with God..1

Spiritual Gifts 9

Prophecy 26

Prophetic Components 33

Judging Prophetic Words 59

Get Ready To Prophecy 64

What To Do With Seemingly Negative Words 74

Growing In The Prophetic 84

Prophetic People & Prophets 93

MSN Ministries 102

• CHAPTER 1 •

Friendship with God

AS WE WALK THROUGH THIS BOOK together, I am going to touch on very practical topics that will help you in the prophetic ministry. That said let's remember to put first things first: Friendship with God. Intimacy with God is the essential thing in our lives. We want to grow in our relationship with the Lord. Growing in knowing the Lord was Paul's prayer for all of us!

"May Christ through your faith [actually] dwell (settle down, abide, make His permanent home) in your hearts! May you be rooted deep in love and founded securely on love, That you may have the power and be strong to apprehend and grasp with all the saints [God's devoted

people, the experience of that love] what is the breadth and length and height and depth [of it];[That you may really come] to know [practically, through experience for yourselves] the love of Christ, which far surpasses mere knowledge [without experience]; that you may be filled [through all your being] unto all the fullness of God [may have the richest measure of the divine Presence, and become a body wholly filled and flooded with God Himself]!" - Ephesians 3:17-19 AMP

You may have heard this before but it's worth repeating, the essence of prophetic ministry is becoming a friend of God, it's not just giving prophetic words. Jesus stated throughout the book of John that he only did what the Father was doing. We are the disciples of Jesus, His friends, and we want to know Him and do what the Father is doing. Lord speak, your friends are listening! At the same time, we don't seek the Lord strictly for information. What husband or wife would want their spouse to be with them just for the information they could provide?

We seek to know Him because He is worth knowing. We aim to love Him because He first loved us. We want all ministries to flow out of intimacy with God especially prophecy. Our goal is to know and love Him! Amen (Phil 3:12-17).

It's also invaluable for our own lives to hear God's voice! *"Man doesn't live by bread alone but every word that proceeds from the mouth of God." - Deut. 8:3.* We want to obey the Lord, we want His leading in our lives, and we want to hear His voice. He speaks to us in many ways - through His written word and His voice directly to our hearts by the power of His Holy Spirit. The closer we are to the Lord, the more we will hear and know His will for our own lives. May we all be known as a friend of God, Amen?

"You are my friends if you do what I command. I no longer call you servants, because a servant does not know his master's business". - John 14-16

An accurate image of God the Father

"Pursue love, and desire spiritual gifts, but especially that you may prophesy. For he who speaks in a tongue does not speak to men but to God, for no one understands him; however, in the spirit, he speaks mysteries. But he who prophesies speaks edification and exhortation and comfort to men." - 1 Cor. 14:1-3 NIV.

Prophecy defined is God speaking to strengthen, encourage and comfort others. It's not expressing personal encouragement but Divine encouragement. To prophesy is to hear from God and speak to others. So why talk about your image of God the Father? What does that have to do with prophecy? The reason we have to talk about your image of God is that all prophetic ministry runs through a filter called you! To properly encourage others through prophetic ministry we must be able to communicate the Lord's heart for that person accurately. Tainted images of God can taint the prophetic message from Him. Many of us take a picture of our natural Father and project it onto God. Maybe your father was harsh and punitive, as a result, you perceive your heavenly Father the same way. How might that affect the prophetic words or impression from God you're expressing to others?

I once had a vision of young man eating pig slop. If my understanding of God the Father was punitive, I might have blurted out something like this: "You better stop eating pig slop, or you're going to be in big trouble. Watch out for lighting, God's judgment is going to strike you!" Would that have been a proper representation of what God wanted to do in this young man's life? This vision and information were actually for me, not him. I simply responded, "Oh, Father, I see a prodigal. What do you want me to say, Lord?" It was simple. We know from the Word of God what the Father's heart is towards prodigals. I simply went to him and said, "The Father loves you so much, and He is waiting for you and longing to put a robe on your shoulders and a ring on your finger." He just broke down and began to weep. I asked for the love of the Father to touch his heart. In a moment, he was no longer a prodigal. As a result of knowing his condition, I also knew how to minister to him. If you have something like this happen to you, stop and pray! Ask the Lord what to do with the information He just gave you.

My husband, Stuart and I were pastors of a singles ministry for many years. I would often have dreams about different individuals in the group. In these dreams I would find myself outside the person's house looking into the window of their home, watching what they were doing. In one of these dreams the Lord showed me a young man from our group drinking and very drunk. Suddenly a nurse walked into the home, gave him a shot in the arm causing him to sober up immediately. Of course, the dream was easy to interpret. I was his pastoral leadership at the time, and we had a relationship, so I decided to meet with him. I didn't expose him publicly in the group because that is not the Father's heart.

Let me take a moment to say something on this note. If you don't have a close relationship with someone, but you believe God has given you divine insight, ask Him what you should do with this information. Sometimes I merely pray and other times the Lord will set up a divine appointment, giving me an opportunity to encourage someone. Still, other times the Lord will show me specific situations in cities, nations, regions, and churches for no other purpose but prayer. Again, if you receive revelation from the Lord, take the time to seek Him on what to do with it as well.

I did finally meet with the young man from my dream. I told him that the Lord revealed to me that he was struggling with alcohol, but God wanted to heal him. I urged him to repent and let us help him.

He denied it all and later that week he was thrown in jail for drunk driving. It cost him thousands of dollars in fines and almost his fiancé as well! Eventually, he had to deal with his drinking because not only was he reaping consequences of his own choices but The Lord disciplines the ones He loves (Heb. 12:7-13). Was the prophetic insight for encouragement, exhortation or comfort? Exhortation means to communicate and emphatically urge someone to do something. The Father in His love for this young man was extending His hand of mercy and I was advising him to take it!

It's a sobering thought to realize you are speaking forth a word and expression of God's heart towards others. We can't represent His heart and words accurately unless we have a proper image and understanding of God. We need to know Him and be known by Him.

Activation Exercise

Take time to examine your current relationship with The Lord and ask Him the following questions and write down what you hear:

1. Father, where have I projected on to you an improper Father image? Listen. Write it down.
2. Father, when did you love me and I missed it?
3. Lord, how and where can I make room in my life to develop a deeper relationship with you? Listen. Write it down.
4. If you don't hear anything during these exercises, don't worry. Just pray and allow The Lord to speak to you now or later. The Father wants you to understand who He is and your identity as a son or daughter.

Father, I pray that you would remove wrong images I have projected on to you. Release a Spirit of Adoption over me and help me to renew my mind through your Word. Give me a revelation of the Father's love and secure me in that love. Help me represent your heart well. Help me cultivate an intimate relationship with you. I want to be your friend in Jesus Name, Amen.

• CHAPTER 2 •

Spiritual Gifts

BEFORE WE TALK ABOUT PROPHECY, let's talk about spiritual gifts. The Bible says, *'There are different kinds of gifts, but the same Spirit. There are different kinds of service, but the same Lord. There are different kinds of working, but the same God works all of them in all men. Now to each one the manifestation of the Spirit is given for the common good. To one there is given through the Spirit the message of wisdom, to another the message of knowledge by means of the same Spirit, to another faith by the same Spirit, to another gifts of healing by that one Spirit, 1to another miraculous powers, to another prophecy, to another distinguishing between spirits, to another speaking in different kinds of tongues, and to still another the interpretation of tongues. All these are the work of one and the same Spirit, and he gives them to each one, just as he determines. The body is a unit, though it is made up of many parts; and though all its parts are many, they form one body. So it is with Christ." I Cor. 4:12 NIV.* The Bible also says, *"Pursue love, yet desire earnestly spiritual gifts, but especially that you may prophesy." I Cor. 14:1*

First, all spiritual gifts are precious to The Lord. He has, through Apostle Paul, told us explicitly to seek them, to earnestly desire them! That word "earnestly" in this context means to pursue with zeal, lust after, busy oneself with, and strive! Why does Paul make such a strong statement about spiritual gifts? Does the church still need these gifts today? The answer is yes! The church needs you to pursue spiritual gifts and grow in the ones the Holy Spirit gives you so His Kingdom can advance! What army doesn't need all its soldiers armed and ready? The body of Christ needs all its members to be effective. The church and the world need you to operate in your spiritual gifts!

A few things to remember about spiritual gifts include the following: Spiritual gifts are for the common good, and they are given to help others. They're not badges of spiritual rank or fruits of the

Spirit. As you know, gifting doesn't always equal character, and anointing doesn't equal maturity. So it's important to be humble with our gifts and step out with the measure of faith we have and begin to use them. When we do, we'll grow in those gifts. Also, the Holy Spirit gives gifts according to his divine will! We may not have the same gift someone else does, but that doesn't mean God loves us any more or less. Do not equate gifting with God's love and favor. He loves us all and if you doubt this, look to The Cross. He can't love you any more than dying for you. Let's honor one another and value the gifts that God has given each person.

Why especially that you may prophesy?

"Pursue love, and desire spiritual gifts, but especially that you may prophesy. 2 For he who speaks in a tongue does not speak to men but to God, for no one understands him; however, in the spirit he speaks mysteries. 3 But he who prophesies speaks edification and exhortation and comfort to men." - 1 Cor. 14:1-3 NIV

"But if an unbeliever or someone who does not understand

comes in while everybody is prophesying, he will be convinced by all that he is a sinner and will be judged by all, and the secrets of his heart will be laid bare. So he will fall down and worship God, exclaiming, "God is really among you!" - I Cor. 14:24,25.

Have you ever received a prophetic word? One word from The Lord can change the entire course of your life! What was the fruit of a prophetic word you received? For me, it can bring an infusion of faith and encourage me to believe again. Other times prophetic words will confirm a direction The Lord has already spoken to me. It can also feel like a kiss from the Father as He declares His promise over me, "Cathy, I will never leave you or forsake you." God wants to speak to you and through you.

What about an unbeliever?

Scripture also tells us that prophecy isn't just for the church but a sign to the unbeliever. The Father wants to speak to all His children. Men and women are all created in His image. It's never been "us" (believers) versus "them" (unbelievers). He died that ALL would come into a relationship with Him. The Lord will often speak to me about a perfect stranger. He usually reveals the treasures inside of them, their heart's desires, and their destiny! Usually when I'm done sharing what the Lord has shown me I often get the same question, "Are you a Psychic?" I respond with, "No, I don't know you, but God does." He sees you and wants you to know He loves you. I have seen many people come to Christ when the secrets of their hearts are revealed. We're learning about prophecy, hearing God so that you can begin to discern when God is talking to you and wants to speak through you to others. God wants to speak to you and through you!

Revelatory Gifts

In 1 Corinthians 12:8-10, Paul lists nine spiritual gifts. I am going to focus on four revelatory gifts including word of knowledge, word of wisdom, discerning of spirits and prophecy.

1. Word of Knowledge: Is a specific fact about a person, place or event not obtained in the natural. It

could be a name, occupation, birthplace, a physical condition, and any specific detail. Generally contains no directional guidance, just the facts. In the story of the woman at the well, Jesus tells the woman to go and call her husband. She tells him she has no husband. He says, *"You're right you have no husband now, but you have had five husbands, and the one you're with is not your husband either." - John 4:16-19.* Jesus shared with this woman a "word of knowledge." One time I was at Wal-Mart shopping and looked at a woman and asked her if she had neck pain? She said, "Yes, how did you know?" I had received a word of knowledge and put it in the form of a question. I wasn't confident at the time in this area of hearing God's voice and asking a question lowered my risk of embarrassment. Another time I was walking by a co-worker I looked at her and said, "You're pregnant!" She said, "No, I am not. I did a pregnancy test two weeks ago." Because of what I said she decided to take another pregnancy test and found out she was in fact pregnant.

Words of knowledge can be powerful especially when doing evangelism and praying for the sick. Ask God when you're running personal errands, in restaurants, at work or shopping for words of knowledge and step out.

2. Word of Wisdom: Insight, divine revelation of the will, plan or purpose of God for a specific situation and how to best apply it. A word of wisdom can often be directional. It is divine wisdom. Have you ever had the answer to a situation and you knew that it didn't come from you? Maybe others around you even commented, "Wow that was brilliant." You were thinking the same thing because you know it didn't come from you. It is possible you received a word of wisdom. 1 Kings 3:16-28 tells the story of King Solomon's legendary wisdom demonstrated by a dispute concerning a baby. Two women were fighting over a child, Solomon says let's cut the baby in half and give them each a piece of the child. One woman said, *"Please, my lord, give her the living baby! Don't kill him!"* At that point, Solomon knew who the birth mother was. One example in my own life involved the sale of our home. My husband began to feel strongly we needed to sell our house. I didn't want to sell it, even our pastor at the time told us not to sell it, but Stuart felt it was the Lord. He thought

it was wisdom and felt a sense of peace about it. So we sold our home. Within a month the housing bubble burst. The economy shifted, and people started losing their homes. We were the last home in Mission Viejo, California to sell at the top of the market. Had we kept the house, we would have been upside down losing all our equity. We also had a loan payment we couldn't afford. Even now, more than seven years later the home still has never recovered the same value it had then. We also had no idea my husband would soon have back surgery resulting in a loss of his income which would have made it impossible to continue the house payment. God knew, we listened and obeyed. We also received a promise at the time we sold our home. While signing the papers, the Lord spoke to me, "Your home will come back to you." We have since received prophetic words confirming God wants to give us a new home.

3. Discerning of Spirits: The word "discern" means to "to distinguish between" or "perceive or recognize" and the word "spirit" according to scripture can mean angels, demons, the human spirit, anointing and the Holy Spirit. Discerning of spirits then is the

ability to recognize and distinguish between different types of spirits. Many people see a discerning of spirits as only the ability to recognize if something is demonic, this is just one aspect of this gift. One example of "discerning of spirits" in the scripture is Paul in Acts 16:17-18. A woman is following Paul around crying out, *"These men are the servants of the most-high God, which will show you the way of salvation."* What she was saying was, in fact, true, but Paul discerned it was not the Holy Spirit. He then proceeds to cast the demon out of her.

I remember preaching on the streets, and a demonized Hispanic woman stood in front of me and sang the song "Majesty" by Jack Hayford. The only problem was she interrupted the preaching of the gospel and sang in perfect English, not a language she spoke. After she finished, I simply stated, "Even the demons know that Jesus is worthy of worship!" At that point, she manifested and started spewing all kinds of filthy words at me. So we pulled her aside and prayed for her.

Another time I was praying for a young teenager in front of a pizza parlor. She was a nominal believer at best, forced to go to church by her mother. She heard us praying earlier, came up to me and said, "I want what you have." We said, "We'll ask God to give it to you." At that point she allowed us to lay our hands on her and pray. As we were praying, she began shaking, trembling and then began to jump up and down yelling, "I feel so hot, its like I am burning." This time it wasn't a demon but the power of God! The power and presence of God can show up anywhere even a pizza parlor! Discerning of spirits is a beautiful gift. Ask the Lord for it.

4. Prophecy: Is the supernatural ability to receive information from God about the future. There are many examples throughout the Scriptures. In Acts 21:10-11 there is the story of a prophet named Agabus. He prophesied to Paul telling him that if he goes to Jerusalem, he will be bound and handed over to the Gentiles. Of course, they all felt the prophecy meant Paul shouldn't go. Paul received the information but still went. He knew God's will for his life. Sometimes when we receive revelation for someone, we think we also know what he or she should do with it. Maybe they even ask you, "What do you think I should do?" Unless you have heard insight

from the Lord, don't answer! Simply direct the person to seek the Lord about it. I have had people use me like "dial a prophet" looking for answers. God is the only answer! What was Paul to do? What was he going to say when he stood before the Lord, "I didn't go because of what the prophet said to me?" Paul knew what the Lord had told him and it included suffering for the sake of the gospel. He knew he had to go and told them to stop breaking his heart!

One time Stuart was invited to go to Pakistan. When he got the invitation, I felt the Lord tell me that he would receive all the funds he needed to go. That week we received a check and had the money to purchase the ticket. As the weeks went by, we started to lose our peace about going. People all around us reasoned that maybe it was just our fears; after all, we had the money. We were wondering the same thing. Still no peace, no go. We've learned this is another way God speaks. We canceled the trip. What changed? We have a few ideas but may never know entirely. For some reason, the Lord has us on a need to know basis; He tells us when we need to know! What about the earlier revelation that he would receive the funds to go? That did come to pass, but something also changed along the way. This is an excellent lesson for us all. It's crucial we stay close to the Lord, because yesterday's revelation may not be today's!

How gifts are given

Gifts come in different ways. First, we know the Holy Spirit is the One who gives gifts. You could receive a Spiritual Gift at the time of your conversion or later in your walk with God. One man I know received an incredible gift of healing and a gift of miracles upon conversion. He said it was like God handed a considerable weapon to a three-year-old! Second, we know we can receive them through impartation. For me, I believe the Lord has been speaking to me since I was a young girl but I never discerned it. I always had a longing for God and a struggle with rebellion. In my twenties, with the help of my brother Steve, I finally surrendered my life to Christ. I remember watching my brother move in spiritual gifts. One day I said to him, "Hey, I would like what you have. You hear from God, and He gives you dreams and stuff." He said, "Ok. Let's pray." We knelt down on the living room floor of his apartment, and he simply prayed, "Lord, everything you gave me, give to Cathy!" A few months later I was operating in new revelatory gifts. I also know people who were minding their own business and living their lives for God when suddenly they found themselves moving in a Gift of healing with unusual manifestations like oil on the palms of their hands and their body covered in gold dust. Others pursued spiritual gifts through prayer, fasting and received them.

1. Impartation: The apostle Paul told Timothy "...*to fan into flame the gift of God given him by the laying on of my hands (Tim. 1:6)*. The word gift refers to a spiritual gift. Paul also wrote to the Romans and said, *"I long to see you that I might impart to you some spiritual gift to make you strong." (Rom 1:11)*. Paul knew he had the authority to impart spiritual gifts. I had a dream years ago that two different people- one a prophet and the other a healing evangelist- came up to me, laid hands on me and prayed. Within the year I found myself in an actual meeting where they were speaking, and they both prayed for me and released an

impartation! The one who was known as a Prophet gave me oil from the healing rooms in Spokane, Washington and the Healing Evangelist laid hands on me and declared revival! Within a year I was on the streets preaching and moving in prophetic evangelism.

Later, I also started equipping others and releasing an impartation for the prophetic gifts as well. The Holy Spirit distributes gifts to us, so the Kingdom of God advances! Let me also say this about impartation. I may ask someone to lay hands on me, or I may put my hands on someone to impart a spiritual gift, but it's not magic! Gifts are given by the divine will of the Holy Spirit for the common good of others. I may lay hands on you and ask the Lord to release to you what I have, but it's still up to the Holy Spirit!

2. Prayer: Don't think just because God is sovereign and does everything just as He wills that you don't need to take action. Paul said, "Eagerly desire spiritual gifts." God has a part but so do you! Our role is to pray and ask. There's a man by the name of Mahesh Chavda who was working in a mental hospital.

Seeing people sick and in bondage, he became desperate to see them free. At the prompting of the Holy Spirit, he fasted for forty days. When he was finished he received an incredible gift of healing that he still operates in today! Nobody laid hands on him. The Bible says, "If you believe, you will receive whatever you ask for in prayer" (Matt. 21:22).

The Bible also says, *"You do not have, because you do not ask God"* (James 4:2). Pray and ask for the gifts you want. Also, don't start a forty days fast because I mentioned it as an example unless you know its God. The point here is God loves the humility, hunger, faith and dependency demonstrated through prayer. He's the good daddy and He is just waiting of us to ask! (Mat. 7:11)

3. Pursue: I have a dear friend name Lynn who has a teaching gift. She hears from God but never considered herself a prophetic type of person and wanted the gift of prophecy. One night she had a dream she was interviewing for a job with a known Prophet. In the dream I was coaching her and giving her tips that would help her with the interview. After the dream she started pursuing the prophetic, learning

everything she could about it! She went to conferences and started reading books on prophecy. She grew tremendously in the prophetic and combined it with her teaching gift. Now she has even equipped others in the prophetic. She did exactly what Paul said, "Earnestly desire spiritual gifts, especially the gift of prophecy." She desired it and pursued it.

Activation Exercise

I want to encourage you right now to stop reading and take a moment and ask the Lord the following questions and write down what He says.

1. Lord, show me what spiritual gifts you've already given me?
2. Lord, show me what steps I can take to further grow in these spiritual gifts?
3. Pray now and ask the Lord for the spiritual gifts you desire.

Thank you Lord that I can hear your voice. Lord, I ask for the revelatory gifts of the Spirit that will help me to en-

courage others. Give me boldness to step out and activate the gifts you have already given me, in Jesus name, Amen.

CATHY GREER

Prophecy

Who can prophesy?

"But Moses replied, "Are you jealous for my sake? I wish that all the LORD's people were prophets and that the LORD would put his Spirit on them!" Numbers 11:29 "In the last days, God says, I will pour out my Spirit on all people. Your sons and daughters will prophesy, your young men will see visions; your old men will dream dreams. Even on my servants, both men and women, I will pour out my Spirit in those days, and they will prophesy." Acts 2:17-18

"For you can all prophesy in turn so that everyone may be instructed and encouraged." I Cor. 14: 31 We know the spirit of prophecy is potentially available to all because the Holy Spirit dwells in us (Acts 2:17-18).

Again prophecy is simply "speaking human words to report something God brings to mind." As stated before, prophecy is when any believer speaks an impression that God brought to his or her mind. Simple prophecy is usually in the scope of encouragement, comfort, and exhortation. However, there are deeper levels of prophetic gifting, ministry, and prophets. We'll talk more about this later. Again, we are all His sheep and we hear the Lord's voice (John 10:4). So who can prophesy? Scripture tells us ALL can prophesy!

Discerning God's voice

When we talk about hearing God's voice, the first question that comes to mind is "How do I know if it is God speaking to me?" As we begin to learn and grow in the prophetic, it's important also to understand not every voice is from God. So how do we discern the Lord's voice? First, we have to know Him personally, know His Word, The Bible, and get familiar with His voice! Like a wife knows her husband's voice or a mother knows her child's voice, it requires time and relationship. Second, as stated before, we have to recognize that not every voice we hear is the Lord. We have to understand our thoughts and emotions also speak to us, and the Bible calls this the flesh. We also have to recognize when the devil is talking to us too. I have found that many believers, especially in the United Sates, haven't even considered the voice of the devil a possibility.

Also let's make it clear up front that God would never give you something contrary to His word, The Bible. To discern truth, you have to know the truth, you have to read your Bible. You would think if a person received a prophetic word contrary to The Bible they would toss it out! Unfortunately, that is not the case. Sometimes we want something so bad we can't discern anything else except what we want!

Stuart and I have people come to us and say, "God told me to..." and it's entirely contrary to Scripture. Try as hard as we can to convince them it's not God; we can't because they want something so badly they have given themselves over to a spirit of deception. The thing about deception is you don't know when you're deceived. So occasionally I will ask the Lord, "If I am deceived in any area of my life, show me?"

Don't let that last statement cause you fear. Some people believe more in the ability of the devil to deceive than the Lord's ability to lead. One of my favorite quotes is by Jack Deere from his book: *"A Beginners Guide to the Prophetic"*. He states, 1*"If we read the Bible with the illumination of the Holy Spirit, We will learn to recognize the character of the Lord's voice. In the Scripture, we see that when Jesus speaks to His followers, He does not condemn, nag or whine. His voice is calm, quiet and authoritative.* [1]

Even His warnings and rebukes bring hope. If it is indeed the wisdom of the Lord that is coming to us, it should bring peace if we genuinely listen (Jas. 3:17; Phil. 4:6-7, John 16:33) the voice of the devil does just the opposite: He accuses and condemns us in order to steal our hope and faith (Rev. 12:10.) Voices have different characters. Learn the character of each voice that speaks to you before you attribute it to God."

Discerning which voice is speaking requires the testing of its character and fruit. What is the fruit of the voice you're listening to? Where did it lead? Bad fruit, like depression, confusion and hope-

---

[1] *Jack Deere, The Beginners Guide To The Gift of Prophecy, (Regal Books) Kindle Edition, 754*

lessness in your life is more than likely the result of following another voice! Our culture also has a voice that produces fruit as well. How is the voice of our culture influencing what we do, think and say? I have met women who lead their lives by the voice of Oprah, and the fruit is not always good. We want to hear and discern God's voice among all the others and follow it! I not saying it is always easy to follow the Lord's voice but salvation, peace, love, and joy is much better fruit in the long run! As we grow in relationship with the Lord, we learn to discern the character of His voice.

What about ministry to others? How do we know if it is God? We know by discernment, and good discernment comes by use. We're going to have to believe He not only speaks to us but can also speak through us. It's going to require faith. You're going to have to step out and give prophetic words. You can practice prophetic ministry in small groups, training classes and even in public places. Over time you will begin to discern when the Lord is speaking.

For some of you, the first step is to believe He can use you in this way. Start believing and start practicing today in your own life. Start asking God to speak to you and invite him into your day! I am continually looking for the Lord to talk to me. I can't imagine even going a day without hearing from the Lord. You see I am in love. If my husband never spoke to me, we wouldn't have much of a relationship. God loves you and wants to talk to you. He is madly in love with you if you don't believe me look at the cross!

Activation Exercise

Take some time today and ask the Lord the following questions and write down what He says.

1. Lord, show me a time when you spoke to me, and I did not discern it? Show me a time when I did discern your voice?
2. Lord, show me any place where I may be deceived, believing a lie and reveal the truth to me.
3. Lord, speak to me and show me who you want me to encourage today? Lord, show me how you want to encourage them?

Lord, thank you for speaking to me and through

me. Give me discernment, help me to hear your voice and obey. I trust in your ability to lead me, in Jesus name, Amen.

WELCOME TO PROPHETIC MINISTRY

Prophetic Components

Before we talk about how God speaks let's look at the three primary components of prophecy, which includes revelation, interpretation, and application. I've listened to many people describe their perspectives on each one of these components. I've noted some of their thoughts in this book. However, there is no better teacher than real life experiences. Business school is never the same as doing business in the marketplace, but it can help. I've walked through each one of these components of prophecy in my own life and helped others. At times it's been a painful learning process and other times incredibly exciting! So let's look at these three components.

1. Revelation – Is a message from God. It's merely God speaking, and He can do it in many different ways.

2. Interpretation – What is God saying about the revelation? Simply put, what does this mean?

3. Application – How do I apply it to my life if it's for me? What do I do with this if it's for others?

I can't remember where I first heard this but it is worth repeating, "What good is a revelation with wrong interpretation?" Even if you have a revelation and right interpretation if you don't apply the word rightly, what good is it? Also if you find interpretation and application a challenge, don't discount your God-given revelation. Remember, *"Man doesn't live by bread alone but every word that proceeds from the mouth of God."* Mat. 4:4 I live to hear God's voice. It's important when we get a revelation, we pray for understanding and learn how to apply it. Do we get it right every time? Of course not, but it's ok. God has grace for honest mistakes and is pleased with faith according to Hebrew 11:6. Let's look at the first component: Revelation.

Revelation - Different ways that God speaks

He speaks in so many different ways including angels, dreams, trances, audibly, visions and even showing up in person and speaking! Usually, when I start talking about the different ways God speaks, many people suddenly realize God has been speaking to them for some time.

Remember, this is all about relationship, and He has a lot to say. He desires to express His love to you and work with you in every detail of your life. In Scripture, we see God compares our relationship with Him to marriage and His relationship to the church in the same way. Your relationship with Him is personal and intimate. As you read this list, ask the Holy Spirit to bring to mind the different occasions God has spoken to you in the past. You too may be surprised to discover how often He has been talking to you.

1. The Bible: We can't talk about revelation without talking about the Scriptures. The Bible has more authority than any present-day personal revelation. This statement is so important I want to repeat it. The Bible has more authority than any present-day vision, encounter, dream or any present-day revelation. Seriously, I know people who are running after

prophets because they claim to have a special revelation. People follow them and focus more on the words that proceed from the Prophet's mouth than from God. There is no greater revelation than the Word of God. God speaks primarily through His Word. We know it's our handbook for living. Know The Word, and you'll know the Lord. I remember hearing a story about a young man who went to a prophet and said, "I want a word from God, will you give me one?" He said, "Sure!" and then handed him the Bible.

2. Jesus Appearing: Throughout Scripture we see the Lord appearing to people. At times He appears in dreams or visions, and other times in person (Gen. 18: 1, Exodus 3:2, Exod. 16:10, 33:18-34:8, John 1:14-18, Exod. 16:9-10). I know a man named Sopal who had experienced the Killing Fields in Cambodia and lived. The term "Killing Fields" was used to describe the horrible reign of Pol Pot, a communist leader, who massacred millions of Cambodians. Sopal having experienced so much terror and death was now being called by the Lord to return to the place where he had seen so much tragedy. So he left the USA and

waited in a hotel room to meet with Vietnamese officials for permission to return to Cambodia. You can imagine the fear he was experiencing because of his past. That night the Lord appeared to him, encouraged him and threw him up in the air like a child. The next day he still had the impression of a handprint on the side of his body. The Lord loves us, why wouldn't He appear to His friends? We also know a former Muslim woman who had Jesus appear to her and tell her, "Stop striving, I am the way." More and more stories are coming out of the Middle East from Muslims talking about Jesus and how He appeared to them.

3. Audible Voice: God spoke audibly throughout the scriptures to individuals, groups, and nations (Num. 12:6-8, Gen. 22:11-12, I Sam. 3:14). There is nothing in Scriptures that indicates that He stopped speaking in this way. Sometimes we believe hearing God is for only church leaders or those in the office of a prophet, but it's not true. I have heard the audible voice of God in my life, and it was straightforward and clear. When you hear His audible voice there's no doubt about it! You obey!

4. Internal Audible Voice: This is just as clear as an audible voice but you hear it with your spiritual ears. In a recent book I was reading on prophecy the author gave Ezekiel 14 as an example. I found this story very interesting. The elders sat down before Ezekiel and the Lord gave him a message but it didn't appear to be audible. Sometimes His internal audible voice can be a whisper as illustrated with Elijah (I Kings 11:12).

One time I was talking with a young man outside a movie theater and I heard a small whisper, "He's ready to get saved." It was like God whispered his secret in my ear. I looked at him and said, "When I die and go to heaven will you be there? He said, "I hope so." I simply responded, "Would you like to know for sure." He said, "Yes I would" and I led him to the Lord.

Other times His internal audible voice is loud and clear! We were with a team in Asia and went to a local hospital to distribute blankets. Before going into the hospital, we were told it was strictly forbidden to share our faith. As we walked through the rooms distributing blankets, I heard the Lord speak loudly and with urgency, "Preach the Gospel!" I looked around the room we were in and asked, "Did you hear that? But nobody else heard it. It was an internal audible voice of God. So I yelled out, "Preach the Gospel, right now!" I pointed to the pastor who was Asian and said, "Preach now!" He went on to preach the gospel and share his testimony. Everyone in the room gave their lives to Christ. Stuart looked at me and said, "We have to go back to the other rooms!" So we did, and over 100 people were saved! When we finally stopped, we realized all the doctors, nurses or security guards were gone. It turns out all of them were outside the hospital, proudly showing off their new ambulance to the rest of our team. It was a "Now" moment, and I am so glad we obeyed!

5. A Knowing: Divine revelation can come without an audible or internal voice; sometimes we have a knowing about something we could have never known. For me, this is actually how the Lord speaks to me most often. I know things about people, details and information and I don't know how? This type of revelation can fall under the category of "word of knowledge," but sometimes it is also about

the future. Jesus knew the woman at the well had five husbands. Other times in scripture Jesus knew the people's thoughts (John 4:18, Mat. 22:18, Mark 2:8, John 6:15).

One time I was in a restaurant and looked over at a husband and wife sitting at a table near us. I felt compelled to talk to them and started sharing what God was showing me concerning the business they owned. They were shocked at the things I knew about them and asked me if I would pray for them. Imagine a perfect stranger asking you to pray for them. My husband asked me later, "Did you know them?" I said, "No." He said, "How did you know all that?" I said, "I don't know, I just knew." It was simply a knowing.

Another time I was at a birthday party and a young man and woman I didn't know walked into the house. I went to greet them and said to the young man, "So you're here in California to get married, Congratulations!" Then I thought, "Why did I say that?" He was shocked and said, "Well, I don't know about that?" I had no idea the woman with him was in fact his girlfriend, and he had come to California to propose. A month later they were engaged.

6. Angels: Angels are "ministering spirits sent to serve those who will inherit salvation" (Heb. 1:14). Angels do so many things including delivering us from the enemy, helping us when we are in danger, even escort us to heaven (Luke 16:22). They can appear like humans (Heb. 13:2). They are also messengers that speak on behalf of God, and we see them all throughout the Scriptures.

I have a friend, and their son has seen angels since he was a young boy. Even as a young man he was always aware of the angelic. Many church leaders didn't know what to do with him. Eventually, he started attending a church that recognized his gifts. Sometimes they would even ask him what are the angels doing? He would tell them, and they would direct the ministry accordingly, and people would get healed and strengthened!

7. Dreams: God often uses Dreams to speak to us. For some of us, it's the only time we stop long enough to hear the Lord! Joseph was told not to divorce, Mary the mother of Jesus, in a dream (Matt. 1:19&20). In the Old Testament, we see the life of Joseph filled with all kinds of Dreams! Throughout

the Scriptures, God spoke through dreams to prophets, kings and everyday people like you and me. Some are very clear and direct, but others include all kinds of symbolic language. Symbolic language can be both biblical and personal. Because dreams are symbolic they can be difficult to interpret. Most of our Dreams are about us even when they include others. There are many different kinds of Dreams too. Dreams that reveal heart attitudes, directional Dreams, and Dreams for others. My husband and I often are given direction from the Lord through dreams.

One time I had a very direct Dream about the Middle East. A man named Judah came to me and said, "So you're going to the Middle East?" I said, "No, I am not going to the Persian Gulf!" He pointed his finger in my face and said, "Yes you are and you'll go to other nations too!" That was a pretty direct dream. A year later we were ministering in the Middle East near the Persian Gulf. It is essential you take time to write down your Dreams and pray into them. We'll save dream interpretation for another time.

8. Visions: Visions are glimpses in the spirit. Some are subtle; some are strong and internal while others are visible with our eyes. You may have a simple vision when praying for someone and may not know what it means. Ask the Lord, "What does this mean?" So many people stop at the Vision and never ask the Lord the actual meaning. Visions are often ways the Lord starts to speak to us. As you seek the prophetic, you may find Visions increasing.

I have experienced every type of Vision. Sometimes the Lord tells me what a Vision means but it is directive for me and not something for someone else. When this happens I don't share the vision I minister accordingly. If the Lord doesn't share with me what a Vision means, I will communicate it to the person I am ministering to. Always ask the Lord if this Vision is for you only or for you to share.

Let me give you some examples of different kinds of visions. I was praying for a young man, and I had a Vision in my mind. In the Vision, this young man had a car from the 1950's, and he was filling his gas tank. I had no idea what it meant so I merely told him the vision. As I was telling him I heard the

Lord say, "It's easier to drive a car with gas then to push it." He knew what it meant but didn't share the details with me at the time because it involved a decision he was pushing for which included leaving the state. After spending time in prayer, he realized he was not supposed to move.

Another time my husband was receiving prophetic ministry, and someone shared with him a vision. The vision was a big wheel turning a little wheel turning a big wheel. The person sharing it said, "I have no idea what this means." Stuart said, "It doesn't matter, I do!" It turned out to be the vision of the ministry that was about to start. Resources from here, a big wheel, turns us, the little wheel, into the Nations, another big wheel. The Vision came to pass, and we have been doing it for ten years.

Open-eyed visions are not as common but can happen. I remember waking up because my whole body was shaking under the power of The Holy Spirit. I sat up with my eyes opened, and I saw a picture of the earth like a globe spinning and a light came down from above it, like a beam and shined in one spot. Then I heard a voice say, "Turkey, My open door, to the Islamic nations!" I had no idea why the Lord showed me this except to pray. I did research it as well after this Vision and discovered Turkey is located at the crossroads of Europe and Asia making it a country of significant geographical importance.

9. Trances: One of the best examples of a trance in the Scriptures is Acts 10:34. Here we read the story where Peter falls into a trance, and the Lord speaks, giving him a revelation that salvation is also coming to the Gentiles. Trances can last a few seconds or much longer. Peter was aware of his surroundings but completely involved in an exchange going on right in front of him. I have read stories of people who have fallen into trances, and when they come out of them, they can share vivid details of the encounter they had with the Lord. In 1800 there was a woman evangelist called Maria Woodworth Etter, she was dubbed the "Trance Evangelist." She would suddenly fall into a trance in her meetings. Sometimes those attending would also fall into trances and then come out of them crying out for mercy and repenting because they had seen hell. The only

comment on her trances she made was God would give her power during that time. Thousand were saved and healed during these meetings.

10. Spiritual Senses: Our spiritual senses tend to incorporate with our five natural senses including sight, hearing, smell, taste, and touch. Most people have no problem believing the prophets in The Bible could see things with their spiritual eyes or hear God's voice with their spiritual ears. Seeing visions, without our eyes open, hearing God's internal audible voice, happens with our spiritual senses. What about smell, taste, and touch? I know people who have experienced smell or taste like vanilla or roses in a meeting where the presence of God is invading. During those time others have heard angels singing with the worship team. I've also read stories of people smelling sulfur while taking someone through deliverance ministry. I realize these things may seem a little strange for some of you but remember God's ways are higher than ours (Isaiah 55:9).

11. The Natural World: God uses natural things on the earth to communicate divine revelation and

truths all the time! All creation testifies to His existence (Rom. 1:19-21)! A locust invasion was a message for Joel to an entire nation. God made a point with Elijah through wind, fire, and an earthquake. Jesus used all kinds of natural things to illustrate divine truth, consider the lilies of the field! He still speaks through natural things today (Joel 2:25-27, I Kings 19:11-12, Luke 12:27).

One time I was sitting in my backyard, and I was asking the Lord about the prophetic promises He had given me about the future. I said, "Lord, what about those promises? Did I miss it? Was I wrong in my interpretation?" I soon forgot about my thoughts and moved into the book I was reading called, "In His Face" by Bob Sorge. Suddenly, a hummingbird came down in front of my face. I was shocked! This bird was flying in front of my face so long I thought to myself, "Lord I know this is you. Is this hummingbird going to talk to me?" Go ahead and laugh but I seriously didn't know what to do with this bird! I would turn my head to the left, and the bird would follow me. I would turn my head to the right, and the bird would follow me. Finally, he left. I thought, "Wow, that was strange?" I laughed and asked, "Lord, what are you trying to say?" I heard His voice, "Go get your dream book." Someone had just given me a dream interpretation book with the meanings of different symbols. I quickly searched the book for their symbolic interpretation of a hummingbird. You have probably already guessed it; hummingbirds were symbolic, in this book, of prophetic promises. The Lord was reassuring me once again that He, in fact, had given me those prophetic promises!

Why or how the author of this dream book interpreted hummingbirds in this way is beyond me. Symbolism is not always easy to understand and is mostly subject to the dreamer. But why did God talk to me through a hummingbird, why not just tell me directly? I don't know maybe just because He can. Perhaps He just thought it would make a good illustration for me when equipping others in the future? All I know is God, used something in the natural, a hummingbird, to speak to me!

12. Body Check: Sometimes the Lord releases words of knowledge through our physical body. Our body tells us all kinds of things in the natural. If we are

feeling pain, we know something may be wrong. It shouldn't surprise us that God might use our bodies to speak to us too. I told this once to a team of people before going on the streets to heal the sick. I said, "Pay attention to your body. If you suddenly have knee pain where you didn't before, it could be God telling you He wants to heal someone's knee!" As we were walking through the shopping mall that night looking to pray for unsuspecting shoppers, one man on the team suddenly got knee pain. He was so surprised he stopped and screamed out "Hey does anyone have knee pain?" We were all a little stunned! But you guessed it; three guys were walking by turned around and said, "We all have knee pain, what about it?" We prayed for all of them, and one of them got healed! The Lord can release a word of knowledge in your body so pay attention.

13. Compassion: What about that precious heart of yours? So many times the Lord will lead through the desires of our heart. Sometimes the compassion of the Lord will draw you to pray for someone. Pray! Ask the Lord what to do? So many times I find myself praying for people because like Jesus I am

moved with compassion! A woman came to me one Sunday after service and said to me, "I have such a passion for going to Africa and working with orphans. I cry about it. I want to go but do you think that is God?" Honestly, I did start laughing and said, "How common do you think this is? Does everyone desire to sell everything, move to Africa and take care of orphans?" Of course, the answer is no but I pointed out the apparent desire of her heart could be the leading of The Lord. Her next move was only to walk out all the necessary steps. Start with a short-term mission trip, learn about orphans and what was involved in caring for them. She had to walk it out. If it's the Lord speaking or calling you to something specific the desire will increase not decrease.

Interpretation – What is God saying about this revelation?

[2]"*The interpretation of prophetic revelation refers to properly understanding it. We must gain God's [2]per-*

---

[2] Mike Bickle, *Growing In The Prophetic*, (Charisma House Books), Kindle Edition, 25.

spec[3]tive on the revelatory information before it becomes most beneficial to us." – Mike Bickle, Growing in the Prophetic

Did you hear what Mike Bickle just said? We must gain God's perspective on the revelatory information! In the area of interpretation, we are dependent on the Holy Spirit. It's very common for people to misinterpret revelation. Sometimes God speaks in symbolic or mysterious ways. Jesus spoke to the disciples directly, and they still didn't interpret what he was saying (Matthew 16:5-7).

Many times it was only those who were hungry for God who will discover the true meaning behind what Jesus was saying. It is important when you receive revelation that you ask the Holy Spirit for the interpretation. If you don't get an interpretation, please don't try to figure it out with your natural mind! It doesn't help!

I like what Mike Bickle says, [3] *"Sometimes the grace to receive revelation is not the same grace to interpret revelation!"* There are times when the Lord doesn't reveal the full meaning of the revelation right away,

---

[3] Mike Bickle, *Growing In The Prophetic*, (Charisma House Books), Kindle Edition, 26

but it unfolds over time. For me at times I have no interpretation, but then over time I suddenly realize, "Oh! This is what that means! What the Lord told me three years ago this is it! A word of encouragement can come to help us through a current circumstance, but when we are dealing with prophecy, foretelling, it usually unfolds over time. We may not even have the full interpretation at the time we receive a prophetic word, but then it actually happens, then we can see the fullness of what it meant. Unfortunately, when it comes to prophetic words, many of us have selective hearing, myself included! Selective hearing is interpreting a prophetic word to fit what you want and or filter it through current circumstances. I find many times this leads to hope deferred (Prov. 13:12). Worse yet we can filter prophetic words through our ambition and insecure hearts which can lead to pride.

Also, God's timing is rarely our timing. Many of us get a prophetic word and start to figure out in our minds what we think it will look like in the end. Not only will this cause problem we could miss what God is really trying to say. I have seen people in business receive prophetic words, try to work it out in their own timing and throw out sound business practices and the results were devastating. You can see why Paul had to say to the church don't despise prophecy (I Thess. 5:20).

For a season I found myself running away from anybody who claimed to be prophetic. I thought I don't want to be involved with those crazy people; they are out of balance. I didn't want to associate with them, which is funny because I was one of them. I just told you I thought a hummingbird was going to speak to me! Over time the Lord began to show me that what was bothering me were errors in interpretation and application that seemed to be all around me. I had to repent, let go of my judgments against the prophetic and all those involved. Now, here I am teaching on the prophetic, God has a sense of humor! Don't let your heart become sick over words that have not come to pass or prophetic words that were wrong. Just hit the delete button and move on! Not every prophetic word someone gives you is from the Lord. You're called to test and judge them.

Don't despise prophecy.

If a wrong interpretation can cause so many problems, what should we do? How do you interpret a prophetic word? It is wisdom to write down the prophetic revelation and pray over it asking the Holy Spirit for insight. We are entirely dependent on Him for interpretation. He may reveal it right away or months later. I've had many dreams and didn't understand the meaning. Months later the Lord will suddenly reveal to me what the dreams meant. Write it down! A clear word from the Lord is different. If it's clear; the issue is probably the application or maybe God's timing.

The Bible tells us Joseph had a pretty clear dream that his brothers would bow down to him (Genesis 37:5-36). No doubt when he was bragging about it to his brothers, he thought they would bow down sooner than later. I am sure he never felt the dreams would play out the way it did. If you receive a prophetic word without a clear interpretation, pray and put it on the shelf until you have an interpretation.

Also, The Bible tells us in The Book of Daniel

that the prophet Daniel had a vision and then purposed in his heart to gain meaning and understanding (Daniel 10). He would humble himself fast and pray. Sometimes the Lord gives us revelation without interpretation so we'll seek Him! Since this is divine revelation, understanding must come from God alone. Relationship with Him is vital! If you feel God has given you revelation along with an interpretation for someone, give it. If you're on the receiving end of a revelation or prophetic word and given it's understanding, you are still responsible for seeking the Lord yourself to make sure it's from Him.

Application – what do I do with this word?

The application refers to the wisdom on how to apply the information or revelation you just received. Maybe you have a prophetic word from the Lord with the right interpretation, now how do you apply it in your life? Application of a prophetic word will bring up the questions, when, where and how? When it comes to walking out a prophetic word, especially in the area of direction, confirmation is essential. Most prophetic words should confirm what the Lord is already saying to you!

Once I was given a prophetic word that I would have a radio program answering questions from the listener because the Lord had given me wisdom. I was a bit surprised because God had spoken to me about this and I was asking him for confirmation. Now that I have confirmation, what now? Do I have a radio program? No, I'm still waiting on God's timing. In the meantime the Lord has involved me in speaking over Facebook and social media. I have since been on the radio several times as well. We know that God's timing is best. We know what can happen when we get ahead of God. Sarah tried to fulfill the word the Lord gave her regarding a child of her own. Things weren't moving along fast enough for Sarah. She thought I am too old and it's been too long so it must happen through Hagar (Genesis 16). We have to do our best to pray and seek the Lord for His timing regarding prophetic words.

There are other times when we don't have all the clarity but times when we are required to walk out those prophetic words over our lives. We do our best to listen, step out in faith and wisdom even when we're not sure on the timing. One time I was so concerned about the timing of a prophetic word, I was paralyzed to do anything. Someone finally said to me, "Cathy, God can shut a door as well as open it! Start walking!"

Remember, many are the plans of men, but the Lord guides your steps (Proverbs 19:21, Psalm 37:23). You can't guide something that's not moving! What does it look like to walk out a prophetic word? Well, there's a classic story I once heard about a young man who received a prophetic word that he would receive a sports scholarship to college. Wow, what an incredible prophetic word and a tremendous promise. Unfortunately, he stopped working hard in sports and school because after all, God said he was going to get a scholarship! What do you think happened? You're right, no scholarship. It's not magic. We need to co-labor with the Lord. We need to walk by faith towards those prophetic words, keep doing what we are doing and watch them unfold over time. Trust that God has the perfect timing to bring them to pass.

Activation Exercise

Take some time right now to do the following exercise and write down what you hear.

1. Remember a prophetic word you don't have a clear interpretation and ask The Lord if this was from Him? Wait and listen.
2. If yes, ask the Lord for interpretation or more revelation about this prophetic word. Wait, listen and write it down.
3. Ask the Lord to confirm it through His written word, the Bible. Wait, listen and write it down.

Lord, thank you for all the different ways you have spoken to me. Like the prophet Daniel, I want to purpose in my heart to seek you for interpretation. Thank you for your prophetic promises you have given me. Show me what steps, if any, I need to take to co-labor with you and walk out these prophetic promises, in Jesus Name, Amen.

WELCOME TO PROPHETIC MINISTRY

Judging Prophetic Words

[4]In the book, [4]*"Basic Training in the Prophetic"* author Kris Vallotton listed his guidelines for judging prophetic words. *"The prophetic word must be congruent with the Scriptures and the heart of God (Galatians 1:8). The word has to bear witness with your spirit (Romans 8:16). The fruit of the prophetic word should bring you closer to God and his people (Phil 3:8-10). The interpretation belongs to God, so we need the Holy Spirit to understand the meaning (2 Peter 1:20-21). Some prophetic words unfold over time (Exodus 3:11-12). We always test directional words and submit them to leadership in our lives (Hebrews 13:17)."*

These are good Biblical guidelines, but I would like to add a couple more when judging prophetic words:

---

[4] Kris Vallotton "Basic Training for the Prophetic Ministry" (Destiny Image), Kindle Edition, 992

1. Consider the person giving the word. What is the character of this person? Are they currently walking upright before God? Are they known for prophetic ministry, do they have a track record of accuracy? Not every prophetic word someone gives you is from The Lord. I'm not saying you have to be in the office of a Prophet to prophesy accurately either. This book is written to help you learn, practice and step out, which occasionally means you'll get it wrong. Test every prophetic word and look at the character of the person as well. Remember, earlier I said all prophecy comes through a filter called you. If a person has many open doors of sin in their lives which can lead to demonic influences, their prophetic words can come from a wrong spirit. The character of the person releasing a prophetic word should be evaluated.

2. Prophetic words should lead you to Christ not the person giving them. I had someone tell me they received a prophetic word from a pastor telling her God wanted her to leave her current church and attend his church. This prophetic word caused a lot of confusion for her. First, because it was from a leader and second, she loved the current church she was

attending. This was a form of control and was troubling to her spirit. Confusion is bad fruit. I encouraged her to hit the delete button and move on. Prophetic words should not cause confusion, guilt, shame or condemnation, that's not the Lord speaking. I've also seen ministers from the pulpit say things like, "God, told me the first 100 people with a $1,000 check would receive a special blessing." You may also hear "Give, and you will get a 1,000 fold return." These types of words at times appeal to a spirit of greed. First, God has already blessed you and second, we don't give to get. Yes, I am aware of the "law of reaping and sowing." It could be all that giving is storing up for you a reward in heaven not on earth. Also if you ever hear or receive a personal prophetic word that feels like manipulation, throw it out! Manipulation is not from God.

3. Test those grandiose prophetic words. I find it amusing when people give me words that are incredibly grandiose. Especially when it has nothing to do with what I am currently doing. I am not saying God can't do great things through a life yielded to him. He can, and He does! But don't let prophetic

words tempt you towards pride. Again, let God confirm what He wants you to do and remain faithful to the task at hand. Remember it's all for His glory, not yours. You'll know the false by knowing the real. Spend time with The Lord and in His Word. Again, use the guidelines listed above to judge prophetic words. If you want to learn more about judging a prophetic word, there is a book I found helpful by Jennifer LeClaire titled, *"Did The Spirit Of God Really Say That? 27 Ways To Discern a Prophetic Word"*.

Activation Exercise

Let's take time right now and do an exercise using the guidelines listed above. We are called to test prophetic words. *I John 4:1 "Dear friends, do not believe everyone who claims to speak by the Spirit. You must test them to see if the spirit they have comes from God. For there are many false prophets in the world."*

1. Take a prophetic word you believe God has given you or someone else gave you and test it using the guidelines listed above.
2. Write down the revelation the Lord is giving you

as a result of testing the prophetic word.

Lord, thank you that through the power of the Holy Spirit and the Word of God I can discern the true from the false. Help me to test every prophetic word. Give me increased discernment to distinguish between the Holy Spirit, the human spirit and demonic spirits in Jesus Name, Amen.

CATHY GREER

Get Ready To Prophecy

Let's explore giving a prophetic word. I want to share with you some practical things that will help you hear God's voice, move past any fear and grow in the gift of prophecy.

No room for error?

For many years my husband struggled with the ministry of the prophetic because sometimes the words were not accurate. Part of the problem was his lack of understanding between Old Testament prophets and New Testament prophets. Once we were attending a meeting where the leader was continually giving us prophetic words saying, "We were going to prosper." The more prophetic words we got, the worse our financial situation became. We finally asked the leader to stop giving us prophetic words about our finances or next time we would bring a bag of rocks!

Of course, we were joking because we knew when Old Testament prophets gave words that were wrong they were stoned! We didn't understand what the Lord was trying to say. In the middle of our situation, He was trying to encourage us our circumstances will change. Due to our lack of understanding, we missed the Lord's encouragement.

It's important to understand that in the Old Testament, prophets received a word from God and the fate of an entire nation depended on the accuracy of that word. Old Testament prophets received directly from God, and it was 100% accurate. In the New Testament, praise God, the Holy Spirit now dwells in us (Acts 2). We can now all hear from God. We can all prophesy and speak subtle or direct impressions the Lord gives us. According to the New Testament, we prophesy by faith (Rom. 12:6). Also according to the New Testament, we are all called to judge prophecy (I Cor. 14:9). Old Testament prophets had the whole picture, but the New Testament tells us we only prophesy in part (I Cor. 13:9). You may get a piece of the puzzle, not the entire puzzle.

Right now, picture the most prophetic person you know or even a known Prophet. They still only prophesy in part. Also, it is good to remember we are all growing and maturing in our spiritual gifts. So let's make room for people to step out, practice and grow. Will they get it right every time, no! Again, it's ok, there is grace for our immaturity, and God loves faith!

"Two or three prophets should speak, and the others should weigh carefully what is said." - I Cor. 14:29

"Do not put out the Spirit's fire; do not treat prophecies with contempt. Test everything. Hold on to the good." - I Thessalonians 5:20

"For we know in part and we prophesy in part," - I Cor. 13:9

Get ready to listen

My friend Lynn and I were talking about this subject "Hearing God's Voice." The discussion eventually came around to the reasons why people don't hear. Lynn said, "Cathy, you know one of the biggest reason people don't hear God's voice is heart hindrances." I thought, of course, heart issues block us from hearing clearly from the Lord. Think about it? Can you hear the Lord's leading in your life when your heart is filled with anger? When you're unforgiving, fearful or worried can you hear clearly from God? What if you're striving or your heart is full of jealousy, bitterness or envy, can you hear clearly? More than likely you will not be able to hear.

Open doors of sin give the enemy access to our lives. Deeds of the flesh can block us from hearing God's voice for ourselves and for others. It's important to let the Lord till the garden of your heart on a regular basis for the sake of your relationship with Him. This is something I do daily. Like David said in *Psalm 139:23-24*, *"Search me, God, and know my heart; test me and know my anxious thoughts. See if there is any offensive way in me, and lead me in the way everlasting."*

Also, busyness can block us from hearing God. It is essential to still yourself, wait on the Lord and practice listening. God says, *"Be still, and know that I am God." (Psalm 46:10)* I remember when the

Lord spoke to me and said, "Psalm 46:10 is your life verse." Which for me means I will live the rest of my life from this verse. Being still isn't easy for me. In the context of this verse, God is saying, "I am on my throne. I tell my enemies to be still and my people, be still because I am that I am. When I look at the kings of the earth and nations that rise up against me, I laugh!" The bottom line is this, "I am in control, and in this, you can rest."

But for most of us, it's hard to be still especially in our thoughts, if we are not trusting God. Our lives are engulfed in busyness. Like I mentioned before one reason God speaks through dreams is that for many of us this is the only time we're still. Oswald Chambers said, *"What hinders me from the hearing is that I am taken up with other things. It is not that I will not hear God, but I am not devoted to the right place. I am devoted to things, to service, to convictions, and God may say what He likes, but I do not hear Him."* Busyness can crowd out the voice of the Lord, be still and take time to wait on the Lord.

Giving words of prophecy, naturally supernatural

Have you heard the term "naturally supernatural"? John Wimber, Father of the Vineyard Church Movement, first introduced me to this phrase in the 1980's. John was all about being natural in the context of the supernatural. First, it's natural that we would be supernatural after all we have the same Spirit that raised Jesus from the dead living inside us! We are talking about God himself dwelling in us. It is like running around with power inside that can spill out anytime and heal someone, cast out demons and even raise the dead! We are supernatural.

I realize there are times too when God may ask someone to do something that doesn't seem very natural. When you read about the prophets in the Old and New Testament sometimes they did strange things. John the Baptist went around in camel hair eating locusts, and that's pretty strange. Let's face it, sometimes obedience to the Lord can look strange to those around us. However, let's not be strange for the sake of being strange! When it comes to operating in the spiritual gift of prophecy, we want to be effective and naturally deliver the supernatural. We want people to receive what we have to say. Here are a few considerations when delivering a prophetic word:

1. Don't talk yourself out of prophetic words: I did this for so long. I discounted random thoughts I had and would say to myself, "Oh, that's just me!" Many times the prophetic words, impressions, and visions come when we least expect it. Have you ever suddenly been thinking about someone and an hour later you run into them? One time I looked at a woman and thought to myself, "I wonder if she has a headache?" My next thought was, "Where did that come from?" Instead of discounting this time, I asked her, "Do you have a headache?" and she said, "Yes, I do!" We prayed, and it left!

2. Bad Timing: Scripture says, *"The spirits of the prophets are subject to the prophets" I Cor. 14:32.* The Holy Spirit will usually subject himself to the vessel He is using. In other words, you do have a measure of control. Don't jump up in the middle of the pastor's sermon and shout out a prophetic word, then

later say, "God made me do it!" or "I couldn't help it!" Yes, you can help it. Also, please don't prophesy when you're angry, have strong feelings towards someone or use it to validate your doctrines.

3. Prophecy in the Church: General words during a church service can be very powerful and bring great encouragement to everyone. They can build faith! If you do have a word for the church, submit it to the leadership or person leading the meeting. It is up to them to decide if the entire church needs to hear it. You're only the messenger, but the pastor/leader has a responsibility before the Lord to govern with wisdom. You did your part and gave them the prophetic word! That's it! Trust God to work with His church.

Also, there's no reason to say, "Thus says the Lord!" When the prophetic word is judged, you'll know if it's from the Lord or not! I like to state, "This is what I think I am getting from the Lord" or "I feel like the Lord might be saying this." Even after I give someone a personal prophetic word, I will encourage the person to test it.

4. Prophecy outside the Church: My prayer is you will have many prophetic words for people outside the church. When you do, let's be natural about it. Avoid lots of Christian phrases like "covered in the blood." If I have a word of knowledge, I ask a question. "Do you have a sister you're concerned about?" If they say, "No I don't have a sister." I move on. Let's be naturally supernatural! Also, always ask permission to share or pray for someone you don't know. I like how my friend put it, "They hold the remote." Picture a stranger you're speaking to holding a remote control. If they click you off, respect that decision and move on.

5. Judgment and Warning Words: Remember we move out of love, expressing God's heart when we give prophetic words to others. If the Lord gives you information that seems negative about someone, the information is more than likely just for you to pray and ask the Lord. We'll talk more about these seemingly, negative words in another section of this book. Also, don't tell everybody what the Lord told you about someone else. How would you feel if someone did that to you? Remember, it's the Lord's

kindness that leads to repentance (Rom. 2:4). If you do have a warning word that keeps persisting, submit it to the church leadership.

6. Be Kind: I can't express this enough. Author, pastor, teacher Jack Deere states, [5]*"The Lord's kindness is the standard for all prophetic ministry."* Always give prophetic words with tenderness and humility. We want people to feel the Lord's kindness and love through us. All prophets would do well to ask the Holy Spirit to write the following proverbs on their hearts: *"A gentle answer turns away wrath, but a hard word stirs up anger."* (Prov. 15:1). *"Through patience, a ruler can be persuaded, and a gentle tongue can break a bone." (Prov. 25:15).* If we frame our messages tactfully and avoid attacks on a person's character, our words are more likely to find a home in the hearts of our hearers."

---

[5] Jack Deere, *The Beginners Guide To The Gift of Prophecy,* (Regal Books) Kindle Edition, 1390

CATHY GREER

What To Do With Seemingly Negative Words

Let's tackle the subject of seemingly negative prophetic words. Many teachings today in the prophetic ministry will tell you that if you hear a seemingly negative prophetic word, then it's not from God but is that true? Remember, while attending a meeting I saw a vision of a young man eating pig slop? When you have a vision, pray and ask the Lord for direction. In this particular case, the information was just for me, so I knew how to minister.

Some people teach if you receive a negative prophetic word you should move in the opposite spirit. I once heard one example mentioned by a Prophet who received negative revelation about a man addicted to pornography. Instead of stating what was revealed to him, he moved in the opposite spirit and told the man, "God is calling you to purity." Of course, that would be true and it was the direction he felt God told him to take.

Why are so many people, especially leaders, concerned over any seemingly negative prophecy? Unfortunately, many leaders like myself have experienced people gravitating to the negative due to wounds in their soul. It's from this place they prophesy negative words the Lord is never saying. So for those who are just beginning to step out in the gift of prophecy, they're asked not to release anything negative but only positive encouraging words, after all, scripture says, "prophesies speaks edification and exhortation and comfort to men."- 1 Cor. 14:1-3 NIV.

I understand what some of these teachers are trying to accomplish. However, there are times when prophetic words fall under the category of exhortation. Exhortation means to encourage someone strongly to action. Recently, I was reading a book written years ago by John Wimber titled, "Power Evangelism." In the book, John tells a story about an unusual spiritual encounter he had on an airplane. During the flight, he looked across the aisle at a man and saw the word "Adultery" over his forehead. Shocked, he decided to pray about it, but it didn't get any better. The Lord spoke again and said, "Tell him to end this relationship, or I will take his life." Then the Lord told John the name of the woman involved in the affair. John obeyed and did what the Lord told him to do. He went over to the man and told him what God said to him. The man jumped up and met John in another area of the plane. He nervously explained to John the woman sitting next to him was his wife and he didn't want her to hear what John had said. He went on to tell him everything he said was right. So shaken up was this man he wept, repented and gave his life to Christ. John then encourages him to tell his wife the truth.

There are many lessons we can learn from this story. First, if you had something this direct, how bold would you be to say anything? It took obedience on John's part to give this prophetic word. Obedience to God versus the fear of man is something we all need to walk in. Second, this was a specific revelation with a clear interpretation and an immediate application. If you had received this word based on current teachings in the prophetic, you might think you need to move in the opposite spirit. Maybe you would walk over to the man and say something like, "The Lord wants to bless your marriage, but the enemy wants to destroy it." That would be true, but we all know that it would not have the same impact.

Again, there are times we're called to move in the opposite spirit and other times when the Lord will reveal information only for prayer. He may also show me someone's current condition so that I would know how to minister. You should always ask the Lord, "What do I do with this revelation?" My nephew, Michael, was in a meeting and the Lord spoke to him about a young man who was attending. He went up to him and said, "The Lord is showing me your complacency is going to kill you." Wow, again that didn't seem very positive, a matter of fact that seemed pretty negative. The young man confessed that was where he was at in his life with God. He then repented and got his spiritual life back on track.

What is God's purpose for exposing personal

sin or private information like this? It's always going to be for redemption. In the story with John Wimber, we see God's goodness towards the man on the airplane. God was giving him a chance to repent, restore his marriage and spare his life. The Lord desired to save him. John carried a pastor's heart and a heart of obedience, so God trusted him with the information. It's my desire we would all grow in the knowledge of God and walk in the fear of the Lord. So that we too could carry His heart, be trusted with information that will lead others to repentance.

What about those other seemingly negative dreams, national and regional prophetic words like earthquakes, tidal waves, and judgment words? Well, there's a lot of tension between the "good news" prophets and the "judgment prophets" in the church today. So many prophetic people have predicted earthquakes in California, waiting for it to drop off the map. Some people have given dates and times it will happen. They usually live on the East Coast, and many of them have been wrong. I wouldn't be typing this if they were right because I live in California. No doubt earthquakes are coming to California after all we live on a fault line. Scientists have been warning us about the "big one" for years. It's not a matter of "if" but "when." If you live in California, you carry an earthquake preparedness kit with you and pray "when"there are an earthquake people's lives will be spared. Unfortunately, these types of prophetic words caused us to dismiss anything that is seemingly negative. Worse yet it can cause contempt for the prophetic. However, what if God did want his people to be aware and prepared, would we listen?

Let's look at the New Testament for guidance on these seemingly negative words and dreams. Jesus said, *"Peter the enemy has asked to sift you like wheat, but I prayed for you. When you turn back encourage your brothers"* (Luke 22:31&32). Wow, that sounds like a negative prophecy. Peter, of course, replied, "No way!" No doubt Peter often thought about these words after the fact and held fast to them. We also see in Scripture Agabus a prophet and Philip's seven daughters, prophetesses, along with many others, were predicting and confirming some specific troubles in Paul's future (Acts 21:11). Agabus also predicted a famine that was to come upon a whole region with such authority, the believers prepared so they could help those who would be affected by it (Acts 11:28). Many seemingly negative words or dreams that include earthquakes, tornados and the like can be from the Lord. The Lord can release information to us like this not to be negative and discouraging but to encourage us to take action, pray and prepare.

One night I had a dream that was severely negative. In the dream God was showing me the coming economic storm that was going to hit the US and the effect it would have on the church I was attending at the time. Even more surprising was the phone call I received from the pastor the next day asking me to speak at one of the weekend services. I knew this was the Lord because it was rare that I ever spoke there. So I shared my dream, along with the instructions the Lord gave me in the dream. His loving mercy He was telling us what to do. He made it clear so we would survive the coming economic storm which would require us to hide in the secret place, meaning we had to cultivate our relationship with Him both in prayer and through His word. We had to hold on to Him, His Word, and His promises if we were going to make it. He also showed me people were going to be leaving the church and difficulties would hit not just once but twice. However, in the dream to my surprise, the church building was still standing but in need of repairs. The church would survive.

He also revealed in the dream that we as leaders had failed to prepare the people for these kinds of storms. Basic discipleship in the area of personal devotion and grounding in The Word was missing. We were so busy with the tasks around us we had not prepared the people. Ouch! Time to repent and change. Then the dream came to pass in 2007 and into 2009 when the housing bubble burst, the mortgage storm swirled and the US went into recession. Many people lost their homes and their jobs. Many people left the church as well. God in His mercy was trying to give us leaders a heads up on how to endure the storm, how to prepare ourselves for the difficulty ahead. In times of trouble, it is God himself who is our refuge, our hiding place. It is our secret life with God where He calms our heart, speaks to us, and we hold on to His promises in Scripture.

We are the children of God, and we have a loving heavenly Father. He speaks and will discipline us, help us repent and help us prepare for the future. He also allows us to co-labor with him. He may reveal what He wants to do in your home, church, city, region or nation so you can pray, take action or speak forth His words.

Before we close out this section, let's talk about what NOT to do with seemingly negative prophetic words. First, we don't go around the church talking to others for confirmation leaving a person exposed in a way the Lord never intended. Second, let's not forget we are representing the Father's heart in these matters. If God revealed your sin or heart condition to someone else how would you want them to handle it? Remember when you receive a seemingly negative prophetic revelation ask The Lord what His redemptive heart is for this situation? Then ask Him what you are supposed to do?

Activation Exercise

Take a moment right now and ask the Lord the following questions:
1. Lord, where are you currently releasing your re-

demptive plan in my own life?
2. What do I need to do if anything (repentance, prayer or practical action?)

Lord, show me where busyness has crowded out your voice and the steps I need to take to make room for you. I thank you for being a God of redemption. You came to redeem us from certain death and give us eternal life. Please help me to see your redemptive plan in my own life and the lives of others. Give me understanding and interpretation on even seemingly negative words. Lord, help me overcome the fear of man and speak your words boldly. Give me your heart for those trapped in sin, guilt, and shame. In Jesus Name, Amen

CATHY GREER

Growing In The Prophetic

Pray, practice and risk

If you want to grow in your spiritual gifts, you're going to have to pray, practice and risk. We know faith is spelled R-I-S-K. You can't develop if you don't practice. My husband, Stuart has a deliverance ministry and has now seen thousands of people delivered from demons. He ministers today in a different way than he did when he first started. He has grown in his gift of discernment, faith, and understanding. A golfer knows the only way to improve his swing is to practice. So faith is required for growth! We pray, ask for gifts, and we take them by faith. We step out and risk, to bless and encourage others. I heard a church leader say once, "If you want to heal the sick you're going to have to pray for sick people." The same is true for the prophetic. If you want to prophesy, you're going to have to open your mouth and speak! Faith pleases God (Heb. 11:6).

Immediate obedience

Like Jesus, we can do what the Father is doing because we hear his voice (John 10:27). However, to do this, we have to walk in immediate obedience. The more you walk in prompt obedience, the more He will use you to encourage others. It's a scriptural principle if you're faithful with the little you'll be trusted with more (Luke 19:11-19). I used to minister to hundreds of high school students hanging around the movie theaters on Friday nights. I would take a few people with me. We would buy them pizza, pray for them and give them prophetic words. Before long I had a reputation around the High Schools in the area, and the students named me "The Jesus Freak Pizza Lady."

When I first started doing this, I only had one other person, a young woman named Marisa, who was willing to come with me. She was faithful and was with me every week. At the time she didn't operate much in the prophetic, but she wanted to. I told her to keep praying and ask the Holy Spirit. It was rare but once in a while, the Lord would give her a prophetic word. She was faithful with the measure she had, and then one night it happened! It was like someone turned on a faucet, and suddenly she was prophesying all the time! It was powerful. God was moving in such a fantastic way. We saw many people healed, encounter the love of God and come to Christ. Step out with the measure of faith you have and watch what God will do.

Community

A community is the best place for us to grow in our gifts. Since gifts are given for the common good to encourage others, we need to step into a community. The local church provides all kinds of opportunities to grow in our gifts, including the prophetic. Smaller fellowships or home groups are a great place to practice. If there is a group that prays for others, join it. If there is a prophetic community in the church, join it! You can also participate in your church outreaches and practice "words of knowledge" in your local community at restaurants, grocery stores, and parks too.

In a community, we also have accountability to each other. Accountability is a beautiful thing because it keeps us from stumbling, falling into error, it builds friendships, and it helps us develop Christ-likeness. Lone prophets or prophetic people that are not accountable to any local church can be vulnerable to problems. We want to have integrity in the giving of prophetic words, be accountable to a community and church leadership.

Pitfalls and potholes

As we go down the road of life, we can get stuck in potholes. I define Potholes as disappointments, unforgiveness, temptations or gossip. Potholes are many times seen and can be avoided, but pitfalls are different. Pitfalls, however, are "hidden dangers or hazards." Author and Prophet, Bill Hammon wrote a great book I would recommend reading titled, *"Prophets, Pitfalls, and Principles."* This book goes into depth on the subject of pitfalls with many Biblical examples. I want to touch on two pitfalls that I see people struggle with the most.

1. Fear of Man – Some potholes we can avoid. The fear of man, however, can be a hidden pitfall. The fear of man according to Proverbs 29:25 is a snare and can hinder us in many areas of our life. It will keep you from speaking up. Fear of what others think about you is a problem. None of us should be hindered either by the rejection of men or the praise of men. Fear of man can cause you to prophesy and say things that aren't even from God. Insecurities can also cause you to love the praise of men more than obedience to God. Motives can become mixed due to the fear of man. In the end, if you care more about the thoughts of others instead of what God thinks, you've crossed a line. What other people think is now more important to you, and their opinions are taking a higher place than God. The Bible calls this Idolatry. Repent. There are countless stories in the Bible of harmful decisions due to the fear of man, but there are many benefits and promises to those who fear God. Ask the Lord to root out "the fear of man" in your life.

2. Rejection – Rejection can be a core issue in someone's life regardless of the prophetic. Family history, abuse, divorce, rape, molestation; these are huge issues in people's lives that cause rejection. However, rejection around the prophetic is also common. First, we must recognize that Jesus was rejected and we will experience rejected too. So plan on rejection. Not everyone is going to receive what you have to say. Second, you can experience rejection without caring a "spirit of rejection." Rejection is a pitfall that many have fallen into when it comes to the prophetic. When someone carries a "spirit of rejection" they usually have a "victim spirit" and "a spirit of self-pity" too. If you're in that pit of rejection right now let me suggest you first forgive. Forgive those who rejected you. Also, forgive yourself and God if you need to. Ask the Lord to heal the wounds in your soul and deliver you.

I liken the prophetic ministry at times to being a mailman; this helps me avoid the pitfall of rejection. I might have the job of a mailman, but my identity isn't a mailman. No, it's a beloved child of God. He loves me regardless of what I do. Still, I enjoy being about my Father's business because I am with Him. Another way to say this is you have a gift, but your identity is not the gift. If my Heavenly Father asks me to deliver the mail to you but you decided not to check the mail, pick up mail or read the letter what's that to me? My part is done. I understand those called to the office of Prophet are the gift themselves to the Body of Christ. So when rejected, it can be even more painful. No one said rejection was easy. Still, it doesn't mean you have to carry a "spirit of rejection."

Now there are some prophetic people or so-called prophets that are just broken people with a "religious spirit." These people believe the only test of a true prophet is rejection, they pride themselves on being rejected and hop from church to church. They have allowed past rejections to move into bitterness, then pride. They now are hearing the enemy's voice. The church discerns their prophetic words are not the Lord and rejects their message. They see this as another sign their prophetic word is from God and leave the church. The cycle is then reinforced again and again as they go from church to church. They usually badmouth the church, the leaders, and the pastors. As a result, they have given themselves over to a spirit of deception. There is freedom for these individuals in Christ, but freedom takes humility. If you suffer from rejection, ask the Lord to deliver you and heal your heart.

Activation Exercise

Let's take some time now and ask the Lord to search our hearts. Ask him these questions and write down what He shows you:

1. Lord, reveal to me if I am operating in a "Spirit of Rejection?"
2. Repent and forgive anyone that comes to your mind during this time.
3. Lord, show me where I have allowed the "Fear of Man" to control me in any way. Forgive anyone that comes to your mind.

Father, I thank you that I am your accepted and loved child. I am your beloved. Wherever I cared more about what others thought or said over what you think or say, I'm sorry. Thank you for your forgiveness. I forgive myself as well. You said there is no condemnation for those in Christ. Heal me of any deep wounds of rejection. I acknowledge you know just how, when and where you are going to bring about that deep healing in my heart. I rest in the understanding that you are in control of my life. Help me to be still and wait on you, Lord. In Jesus Name. Amen.

Prophetic People & Prophets

Scripture is clear that all can prophesy (I Cor. 14:31). At the same time, Paul talks about prophets too. So what is the difference? A prophet is a calling by God but to minister in prophecy is a gift. In this book, we focused on the gift of prophecy. My husband and I have seen abuse around the prophetic ministry, all over the world. Because of this, I knew I needed to talk about the office of prophets. First, some individuals who frequently operate in the prophetic ministry are still growing in their spiritual gifts. The local churches may recognize these prophetic people and understand they are still maturing in their character. These individuals may be called prophetic people but not called to the office of a prophet.

True Prophets

"And He Himself gave some to be apostles, some prophets, some evangelists, and some pastors and teachers, for the equipping of the saints for the work of ministry, for the edifying of the body of Christ," Ephesians 4:11&12. There are still prophets today according to the Scriptures. As Paul states, one of their purposes is to equip the saints for the work of the ministry. They are called by God and operate in a high level of prophetic revelation as well. A true prophet should be accurate in their prophetic words, have a godly lifestyle, love and honor the Word of God. The mark of a true prophet is "godly character." They also have prophetic insight and wisdom. God uses them in powerfully to build up God's people and release His purposes.

I like what Rick Joyner said in his book titled, *"The Prophetic Ministry." "There is no formula or "how to" for becoming a prophet. If God has not called us as a prophet, it cannot be generated by self-effort. We can ask for spiritual gifts and receive them, but the existence of gifts in our lives does not necessarily mean we have an office of the ministry in the church. If the Lord has called us to a certain ministry, it will be evident in the right season."* *"Not everyone is called to the office of prophet, but the whole church as a unit is called to be a prophet to the world, manifesting Christ's ministry as the spokesman for God."* I agree, let us all become a prophet to the world!

If you believe that God has called you to a particular ministry, it's true that over time it will become evident to all. Many people have called themselves to the office of prophets, but no one else has. If you were called as a Prophet let the Lord confirm it, help you grow and then over time men will confirm it too.

False Prophets

"Watch out for false prophets. They come to you in sheep's clothing, but inwardly they are ferocious wolves. By their fruit, you will recognize them. Do people pick grapes from thorn bushes or figs from thistles? Likewise, every good tree bears good fruit, but a bad tree bears bad fruit. A good tree cannot bear bad fruit, and a bad tree cannot bear good fruit. Every tree that does not bear good fruit is cut down and thrown into the fire. Thus, by their

fruit, you will recognize them.

"Not everyone who says to me, 'Lord, Lord,' will enter the kingdom of heaven, but only he who does the will of my Father who is in heaven. Many will say to me on that day, 'Lord, Lord, did we not prophesy in your name, and in your name drive out demons and perform many miracles?' Then I will tell them plainly, 'I never knew you. Away from me, you evildoers!' – Matthew 7:15-22

A false prophet is not someone who gives a wrong word. A wrong prophetic word may reveal an immature person trying to exercise their gifts. We're also not talking about false prophets outside the church like psychics who get their information from another source. We're talking about false prophets in the church. Author and pastor, Jack Deere writes, *"There is a spiritual prophet who is mature in his gifting and character. There is the immature but growing prophet whose character and gifting are improving. There is the carnal prophet who may be very gifted, but whose character deficiencies produce more strife than the fruit of the Spirit. In terms of gifting the immature prophet and the carnal prophet may look similar; it is only by the spiritual gift of discernment or by evaluating their ministries over time that we can distinguish between them."* I agree that carnal prophets can be a big problem in the church and false prophets are carnal ones.

The Scriptures makes it clear how we tell a false prophet from a true one. Jesus said that we would recognize a false prophet by the fruit of their ministry, not by their power, miracles or accuracy (Mat. 7:15-23). Once my husband and I were traveling oversees and when we returned to the church where we were serving we discovered a false prophet had come in. Many were surprised and asked me, "How can this person be a false prophet when he was so accurate in most of his prophetic words?" Eventually, it became evident to all. The fruit of his ministry was fear, pride, self-promotion, and greed. Unfortunately it was not discerned before he took a lot of money to build his ministry.

Read Jude 4-19; this will help you discern a false prophet. Many have taught in depth on this topic, but I will touch on it quickly. Check the prophet is the motive "the way of Cain" which means, do they operated from anger and rejection? (Genesis 4). Do they "Go the way Balaam"? (Numbers 22-24), which was greed and immorality. Do they go the way of "Korah's rebellion" (Numbers 16), which was the envy of anointed leaders?

Jack Deere writes, *"False prophets ministries are characterized by immorality, monetary gain, rejection of authority, selfishness, manipulation, grumbling, fault finding, flattery, empty boasting and they are a disappointment of all who trust them. This description fits not just false prophets but false apostles, teachers, and elders too."* We will know false prophets by their character and fruit.

Let The Gardener do His work

What about you? You love God right? The Bible tells us that sin in any area of our lives such as anger, unforgiveness, lust, sexual immorality, perversion, hatred, violence, envy, jealousy, selfish ambition, occult practices, idolatry, greed or blasphemy can open door to demonic influence in our lives (Col. 5:11, Gal. 5:19-21). All of these things keep us from a true relationship with God. Remember our main goal is to become a friend of God, not necessarily to give a prophetic word. Allow the Lord to weed the garden of your heart periodically! David prayed this prayer, and I pray it often too, *"Search me, O God, and know my heart; Try me and know my anxious thoughts; And see if there be any hurtful way in me, And lead me in the everlasting way." Psalm 139:23,24.* The Bible says, *"the word is like a two-edged sword" it cuts to the heart of the matter* (Heb. 4:12). It keeps us in truth and out of deception. It also reveals the heart, character, and nature of God. Read your bible daily. Also, abide in the vine, spend time in His presence and cultivate your relationship of intimacy with Him (John 15:9). Let us all value Him more than the ministry.

Welcome to the prophetic ministry. You've only taken the first few steps. God is always speaking, and He wants to talk to you and through you. Jeremiah 3:33 reads, *"Call to me and I will answer you and tell you great and unsearchable things you do not know."* It's my hope this book has helped you understand how to hear God's voice for yourself and for others. His voice changes everything!

Recommended reading and encouragement

Below is a list of recommended reading to help you grow in understanding prophetic ministry. I'm thankful for the people who God has used to bring about a restoration of the prophetic ministry to the Body of Christ. I'm also grateful for the many that have mentored me personally or through their books. I want to encourage you again to desire spiritual gifts especially the gift of prophecy. I also would like to invite you to become a friend of God and to grow in the knowledge (experiential knowing) of Him. To know him is to love him more.

My prayer for you is the same as Paul's, *"I keep asking that the God of our Lord Jesus Christ, the glorious Father, may give you the Spirit of wisdom and revelation, so that you may know him better. I pray that the eyes of your heart may be enlightened in order that you may know the hope to which he has called you, the riches of his glorious inheritance in his holy people, and his incomparably great power for us who believe. That power is the same as the mighty strength."* (Eph. 1:17-19) Amen!

"A Beginners Guide To The Gift of Prophecy" Jack Deere
"Growing In The Prophetic" Mike Bickle
"Prophetic Series, (Three Volumes)" Bill Hammon
"Prophetic Ministry" Rick Joyner
"You May All Prophesy" Steve Thompson

WELCOME TO PROPHETIC MINISTRY

"Basic Training In The Prophetic" Kris Vallotton
"Prophetic Series" Graham Cooke
"Power Evangelism" John Wimber
"The Heart of the Prophetic" Jennifer LeClaire
"Dealing With The Rejection and Praise of Man" Bob Sorge

"Follow the way of love and eagerly desire gifts of the Spirit, especially prophecy." I Cor. 14:1

CATHY GREER

MSN Ministries

Established in 2008, Mission Support Network (MSN Ministries) is a missions organization with a passion for Jesus and His global harvest. We exist to disciple nations according to Matthew 28:18-20. We carry out our mission by working with indigenous apostolic leaders to advance the Kingdom of God through church planting, equipping pastors and leaders, preaching the gospel, ministering to the poor and demonstrating the Kingdom of God in power.

Over the years MSN Ministries has developed relationships with various apostolic leaders and individuals around the world. Together, along with our partners here in the U.S., God's Kingdom advances throughout the nations. Your partnership makes the difference. Please consider becoming a monthly partner today.

WELCOME TO PROPHETIC MINISTRY

About our founders

Stuart Greer - Stuart is a co-founder along with his wife Cathy of Mission Support Network. Pastor Stuart has ministered freedom through deliverance prayer with individuals for years and has now seen thousands set free in Jesus name. He is a gifted teacher and has trained hundreds of pastors and leaders. He has ministered to pastors, leaders, and congregations around the world including Canada, Germany, Mexico, Dominican Republic, Puerto Rico, South Africa, Mozambique, Ghana, Togo, Kenya, Uganda, Russia, Thailand, Cambodia, Vietnam, Columbia, Venezuela, India, Germany and the US. Stuart has a passion for church planting here and in the nations. He served on the board of Jesus Center Church in Torrance, California was an Associate Pastor at Blessed International in Anaheim, California and is the author of "Freedom, Healing & Deliverance" a practical manual for setting others free. He currently serves on the board of MSN Ministries.

Cathy Greer - Cathy is the founder along with her husband Stuart of MSN Ministries and currently serves as the President. She is an ordained minister and has trained many pastors and leaders around the world. Her desire is to see the Kingdom of God advance through church planting, evangelistic outreach, and education for the poor. Cathy is anointed speaker, moves powerfully in the prophetic and has spoken over many influential leaders impacting their lives. She is an author and a Mother in The Faith to many forerunners and catalysts in this generation all around the world. She has a passion for seeing others walk in the fullness of their identity and inheritance in Christ. Cathy has served as a pastor on staff at both Blessed International in Anaheim, California and Vineyard Community Church, Laguna Niguel, California. She is the author of this book and the author of the book, "A Quick Guide To Dream Interpretation."

Give online or by mail Website: www.msnministries.org By Mail: 25108 Marguerite Pkwy, A136, Mission Viejo, CA 92692

Made in the USA
Middletown, DE
14 February 2025